WALTER LANTZ

Woody Woodpecker ®

Takes a Trip

Story by ANN McGOVERN

Pictures by AL WHITE AND BEN DE NUNEZ

GOLDEN PRESS

Western Publishing Company, Inc.

Racine, Wisconsin

Seventh Printing, 1976

Woody Woodpecker sat in the middle of a pile of boxes, bags and barrels.

"I'm tired of my job," he sighed. "All day I make holes in life preservers. All night I make holes in doughnuts. What I need is a change. I need a long, long sea voyage. And that's what I shall have."

Splinter and Knothead were thrilled when they heard Woody's news.

"Sailing, sailing over the bounding waves," they sang.

"Not so fast," Woody said. "First we have to find the right boat to sail on."

They walked down to the harbor to look at boats.
There were blue boats and new boats. Old boats and
coal boats. Boats that looked a frightful sight, but
no boat that looked exactly right.

Except for one. And that boat was big and beautiful and seemed seaworthy. They walked closer to have a better look and Woody fell right over the long legs of a long-faced Captain.

The Captain was moaning and groaning, "My beautiful boat is big and seaworthy. But my beautiful boat is no good. No one will want to sail on such a boat."

"Don't say that, Captain," Woody said. "We want to sail on your boat. We want to take a long, long sea voyage."

"It's nice of you to try to cheer me up," the Captain said. "But just look at that boat. The shipbuilder forgot to put in the windows. There are no portholes! If people sailed on that boat, they wouldn't be able to breathe. No air can get in."

Splinter looked at Knothead sadly. Knothead looked at Splinter sadly. They both looked at Woody, who was smiling from ear to ear.

"Captain, this is your lucky day!" Woody cried. "Look at me! I'm a woodpecker. I can make holes in trees and telephone poles. I can make holes for dough-nuts and holes for life preservers. So why can't I make holes for your boat, too?"

The Captain raised his head. The Captain nodded his head. The Captain *stood* on his head—for pure joy!

And it was no sooner said than done.

Rat-a-tat-tat. Woody made portholes in the port
side.

Rat-a-tat-tat. Woody made portholes in the star-
board side.

Rat-a-tat-tat. He made portholes in the stern and
he made portholes in the bow.

He made dozens and dozens of portholes until the
Captain cried, "Stop! This boat will be nothing *but*
portholes!"

Woody beamed with pride as he looked at his work.
"There are no finer portholes in any ship," he said.

"You have made me the happiest captain in the whole wide world," the Captain said. "I want to make you happy, too. You shall have your long sea voyage. Meet me here tonight when the moon comes up and we will sail across the sea."

They ran home to get ready. In a flash, Woody packed a big suitcase. In a twinkling, Splinter and Knothead packed their suitcases, too.

They turned off the lights, locked the door, left a note for the milkman—and were off.

The boat was big, and perfect for playing games.
Splinter and Knothead played leapfrog over the deck
chairs, over the lifeboats, over each other.

They played hide-and-seek in the bedrooms called *staterooms*, in the kitchens called *galleys*, and in the boat's elevators and swimming pools.

Meanwhile, Woody helped the Captain. He fiddled
with the weather instruments and faddled with the
compasses. He fiddled and faddled too much.

Woody helped the Captain steer the big boat. He fiddled the big wheel to the right instead of the left. He faddled the big wheel to the left instead of the right. He fiddled and faddled too much.

So one day...

"Help! Help, oh help!" the Captain cried. "Iceberg ahead!"

Woody, Splinter and Knothead peered out of the portholes. Closer and closer loomed a mountain of ice!

"My boat!" the Captain cried. "My beautiful boat with its beautiful portholes will be smashed to smithereens."

The Captain began to cry.

"I can make holes in trees and telephone poles. I can make holes for life preservers and holes for doughnuts. I can make a hole in an iceberg big enough for a boat to pass through."

The Captain raised his head. The Captain nodded his head and laughed. The Captain *stood* on his head— for pure joy!

And it was no sooner said than done.

Rat-a-tat-tat. Woody drilled a small hole.

Rat-a-tat-tat. Woody drilled a bigger hole.

Rat-a-tat-a-tat-a-tat-a-tat-a-tat-a-tat-a-tat.
Woody drilled a big, huge, gigantic hole and the boat
sailed right through the big hole in the iceberg.

"Hurrah!" the Captain shouted. "Hurrah for the porthole maker. Hurrah for the iceberg breaker! Hurrah for Woody Woodpecker!"

From the North Pole they sailed to the South Pole. They would have sailed to the East and West Pole, but there aren't any such places.

If ever on a Sunday, you happen to find yourself at the South Pole, you might see penguins and seals playing horse-shoes with rings made of ice. They will tell you (in penguin and seal talk) that the ice rings were made by a certain woodpecker, by the name of Woody, who happened to pass by one day.